DR XARGLE'S
BOOK OF
EARTH MOBILES

Southwark
Council

DULWICH LIBRARY
368 Lordship Lane
London SE22 8NB

www.southwark.gov.uk/libraries   @SouthwarkLibs

Southwark
Council

Please return/renew this item
by the last date shown.
Books may also be renewed by
phone and Internet.

A Red Fox Book

Published by Random House Children's Books
20 Vauxhall Bridge Road, London SW1V 2SA

A division of Random House UK Ltd.
London Melbourne Sydney Auckland
Johannesburg and agencies throughout the world

First published by Andersen Press Ltd 1991

Red Fox edition 1993

3 5 7 9 10 8 6 4 2

Printed in China

RANDOM HOUSE UK Limited Reg. No 954009

ISBN 0 09 988150 0

DR XARGLE'S
BOOK OF
EARTH MOBILES

Translated into Human by Jeanne Willis
Pictures by Tony Ross

Red Fox

Good morning, class. Today we are going to learn how earthlings travel.

Earthlings can reach a top speed of one mile in three minutes in their vest and pants.

The oldest form of transport known to them is the
Dobbin.

To catch a Dobbin, put a square of sugar on your
hand and creep towards him. Grab his hairdo and
fling your legs in the air.

When startled Dobbins do a handstand.

This earthlet is able to travel at many miles per hour down a steep slope. He has attached wheels to his footwear, but no brakes.

Here he is again in the casualty department.

The bicycle is popular. The earthling must hang on
to the prongs and move his knees up and down.

He must put a metal clip around his leg to prevent the bicycle eating the trouser.

Earthhounds can run as fast as a bicycle with pigmeat in. If one approaches, press the ting-a-ling and prepare to eject.

A car has many eyes. It winks at its friends with these. It has a tail. Out of this comes stinkfume.

Every Sunday, the earthling strokes the car with a piece of soft material. He lies underneath it and tickles its tummy. For Christmas, he buys it two woolly cubes with dots on.

If someone bumps the car, the earthlings must go out and wave his fist in the air. He then calls the other earthling the son of a baboon and insists that he buys some spectacles.

A boat is made from a tree and a sheet tied to a stick with string.

When the ocean is bouncy, the earthlet goes green.

Here are some phrases I would like you to learn.
"Yo ho ho and a glass vessel with rum in it!"
"Hello sailor!"
"Earthling overboard!"

An aeroplane has a tail, some wings and a beak but no feathers.

The earthlings are only allowed to get on if they smile. Then, they are tied to the chairs so they can't escape.

If the earthlings stop smiling, they are made to eat leather in glue, boiled plants and a cake with squashed flies in it. A tinful of boiling water and leaves is then poured over their knees.

A train is a long metal tube stuffed with earthlings.

When the train starts, the earthlings on the seats cover themselves with newspaper. The others swing from the ceiling.

Sometimes a family of moohorns have a picnic on the metal rails. The earthlings lean out of the window and shout at the moohorns and the driver.

Then along comes the Tickets Please. He gets out
his snipper and ruins the tickets.

That is the end of today's lesson.
Get into the spaceship quickly and put on your
disguises. We're going to visit planet Earth and have
a ride on a train.

Matron has managed to book us tickets for the
Ghostie Express.

Some
bestselling Red Fox
picture books

THE BIG ALFIE AND ANNIE ROSE STORYBOOK
by Shirley Hughes
OLD BEAR
by Jane Hissey
OI! GET OFF OUR TRAIN
by John Burningham
DON'T DO THAT!
by Tony Ross
NOT NOW, BERNARD
by David McKee
ALL JOIN IN
by Quentin Blake
THE WHALES' SONG
by Gary Blythe and Dyan Sheldon
JESUS' CHRISTMAS PARTY
by Nicholas Allan
THE PATCHWORK CAT
by Nicola Bayley and William Mayne
MATILDA
by Hilaire Belloc and Posy Simmonds
WILLY AND HUGH
by Anthony Browne
THE WINTER HEDGEHOG
by Ann and Reg Cartwright
A DARK, DARK TALE
by Ruth Brown
HARRY, THE DIRTY DOG
by Gene Zion and Margaret Bloy Graham
DR XARGLE'S BOOK OF EARTHLETS
by Jeanne Willis and Tony Ross
WHERE'S THE BABY?
by Pat Hutchins